YEAR OF THE JUNGLE

BY SUZANNE COLLINS

Illustrated by
JAMES PROIMOS

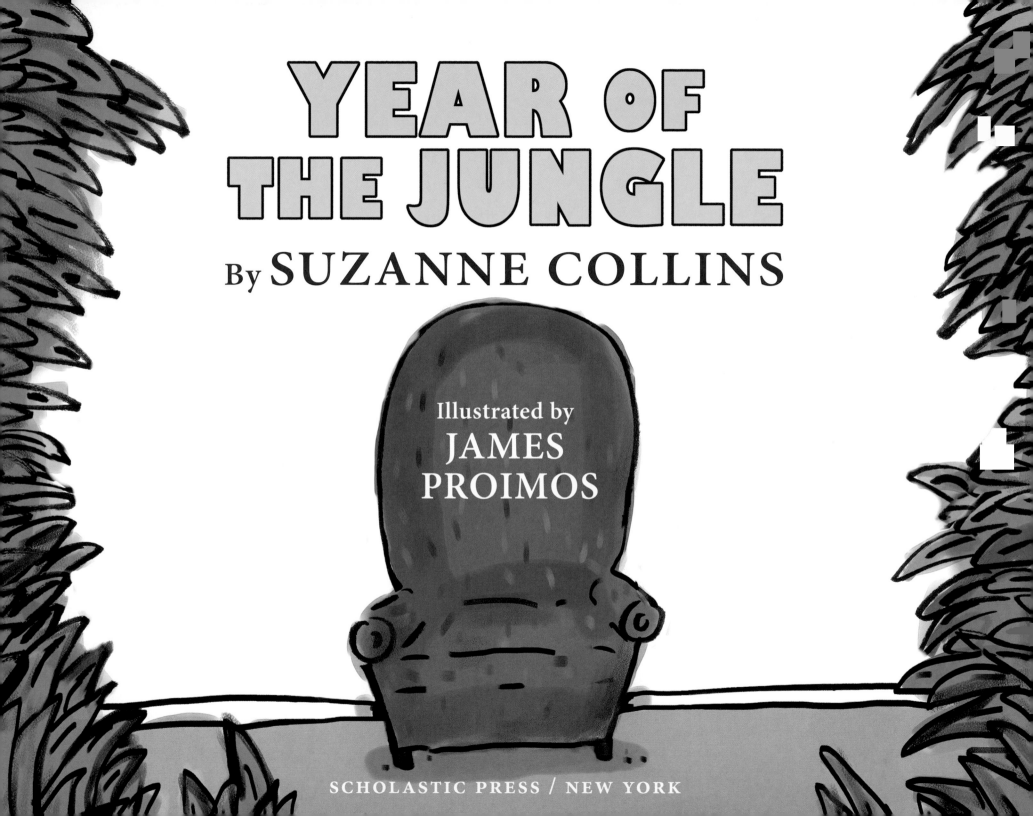

SCHOLASTIC PRESS / NEW YORK

Library of Congress Cataloging-in-Publication Data

Collins, Suzanne.

Year of the jungle / by Suzanne Collins ; illustrated by James Proimos.

— 1st ed.   p. cm.

Summary: Suzy spends her year in first grade waiting for her father, who is serving in Vietnam,

and when the postcards stop coming she worries that he will never make it home.

ISBN 978-0-545-42516-2

1. Children of military personnel—Juvenile fiction. 2. Vietnam War, 1961–1975—Juvenile fiction.

3. Separation (Psychology)—Juvenile fiction. [1. Fathers and daughters—Fiction. 2. Soldiers—Fiction.

3. Vietnam War, 1961–1975—Fiction. 4. Separation (Psychology)—Fiction.]

I. Proimos, James, ill. II. Title.   PZ7.C6837Ye 2013   813.6—dc23   2012015346

10 9 8 7 6 5 4 3 2 1   13 14 15 16 17

Printed in China 38

First edition, September 2013

The display type was set in Gill Sans Ultra Bold · The text was set in Minion Pro

The art was created using ink and Corel Painter

Book design by Elizabeth B. Parisi

For our families

— S.C. and J.P.

My dad reads me poems by a man named Ogden Nash. My favorite is about a dragon named Custard. Even though he always feels afraid, he is really the bravest of all. And that's what makes him special.

We're all something special.

Rascal's the cat.

Kathy's the oldest.

I'm the youngest.   Drew's the boy.   And Joanie's the only one

with brown eyes like my dad's.

Like melted chocolate.

My dad has to go to something called a war. It's in a place called Viet Nam. Where is Viet Nam? He will be gone a year. How long is a year? I don't know what anybody's talking about.

Then someone says he'll be in the jungle. My favorite cartoon character lives in a jungle. He has an elephant and an ape for friends and he bangs into trees a lot.

Rascal and I want to go to Viet Nam, too. You can fly anywhere in your dreams....

We keep an eye on my mom.
Just in case she's thinking
about going to the jungle, too.

But she's always home with us.

Then our first postcards come. Kathy reads mine to me because it's in cursive.

Dear Suzy,
This is a picture of a deer. Don't let Rascal see it. He might think he is a tiger & want to eat it.
Dad

A few days later, first grade begins. I have a new lunch box with its own thermos, and a friend named Beth.

On Sundays, my dad always read me the comics. Drew does it now, since he is the man of the house.

More postcards come from my dad. Sometimes grown-ups ask what he does. When I tell them he's in Viet Nam, they act funny. Sad or worried or angry.

For Halloween, my mom makes me a snow-leopard costume. One of those worried ladies says, "Your dad will be just fine," and gives me way too much extra candy. I start to feel worried, too.

Beth and I trace our hands
and make Thanksgiving turkeys.

Has it been a year yet?

I get a postcard of a man fishing in Viet Nam.

Behind him I can see the edge of the jungle.

It looks different from my dreams.

Dear Suzy,
How do you like first grade?
Do you have a lot of homework?
I'll bet you don't have a lot of time
to tease the cat.
    Love,
    Dad
    xx

Mom and Drew get a tree. Rascal and I rearrange the manger several times a day. He likes to knock over the sheep with his paw. If I knock one over, it annoys him. Does that count as teasing?

My dad sends me a beautiful Vietnamese doll and a fancy silk card with Mary and angels and the Baby Jesus on the front. Inside it reads:

Merry Christmas, Little Sue,
Don't feed Rascal too much turkey.

I wish I could be there to watch you open presents.
Your loving father.

My mom gets a pretty silk card, too, but hers has something stamped on the back. A picture of a soldier with a bugle and a gun. He's in the jungle. Under him are the words:

SOUVENIR OF VIETNAM

It's snowing and I get a birthday card. My birthday isn't until summer. The card should be for Joanie. My mom says my dad's busy and just got confused.

The jungle must be a very confusing place for him to make such a serious mistake.

Candy hearts.

No postcards.

Shamrocks.

No postcards.

Colored eggs.

No postcards.

A year goes on and on.

Finally, some postcards show up.

I wanted one of the jungle.

Instead, I get a city called Saigon.

Dear Little Sue,
How do you like being in first grade? Study hard and when you're home, don't bother Rascal so much.
Pray for me.
    Love,
    Dad

Pray for me?

In May, I make my first communion and I pray very hard for my dad to come home. He doesn't.

I fix Rascal a plate of crayons but, as usual, he won't eat them. From the TV, I hear the words "Viet Nam," and I look up.

Explosions.

Helicopters.

Guns.

Soldiers lie on the ground. Some of them aren't moving.

My mom runs across the living room and turns off the TV.

"It's okay. Your dad is okay," she says. I don't say anything.

Later, I hide in the closet and cry.

Sometimes it's hard to remember what my dad looks like. I stare into Joanie's melted-chocolate brown eyes to try and find him.

The postcards stop coming. I dig out a really old one of a kitten and pretend it's new.

Summer vacation begins. My swimming teacher throws me in the deep end and I nearly drown because he never taught me how to swim. Kathy wraps me in a towel and won't let him near me, even to apologize. So many things are scary now.

Maybe my dad is lost in the jungle. Maybe he can't get out. Maybe he never will. How long is a year? A year is long.

Then suddenly my dad's home.

He looks different. Tired and thin and his skin has turned the color of pancake syrup.

He gives me a bracelet

with tiny bells that really ring.

He gives Rascal a pat.

Rascal and I stand in the doorway watching him. He stares into space. He is here but not here. He is back in the jungle. I need to tell him that I know. About the jungle. About the things that happen there. The words are hard to get hold of. "Rascal didn't think you were coming back," I say finally.

My dad sees us and says,
"You tell him that most people
come back. And I'm home now."

It's true. He's home now. Some things have changed but some things will always be the same.

My dad reads me poems by a man named Ogden Nash. My favorite is about a dragon named Custard. Even though he always feels afraid, he is really the bravest of all.

And that's what makes him special.

Here is author Suzanne Collins in 1968,

the year her father was deployed in Viet Nam.